Little BIG Sister

For my big brother Paul, who introduced
me to the music of David Bowie
E C

For Jacob, Mum & Edward
C I

First published in 2023
by Little Island Books,
7 Kenilworth Park, Dublin 6w, Ireland

Text © Eoin Colfer 2023
Illustrations © Celia Ivey 2023

The author has asserted his moral rights

Designed and typeset by Louise Millar
Printed in Poland by Skleniarz

ISBN: 978-1-91507-105-7

Little Island has received funding to support this book
from the Arts Council of Ireland / An Chomhairle Ealaíon

EOIN COLFER

Little BIG Sister

Celia Ivey

Little Island
Books create waves

Starr and Babes were sisters.
They did everything together.

Starr loved to draw crayon pictures
of her favourite toys.

Babes loved to eat the crayons.
Blue was her favourite flavour.

Sometimes the sisters did things they were not supposed to do, like riding Starr's skateboard indoors.

Or climbing on the furniture.

Or both together.

They especially liked climbing up to the kitchen cupboards where their mum hid treats up high.

Mum said they were like squirrels. They could climb onto anything. Except...

7

... the apple tree in the garden where the treehouse was.

They just couldn't get up the tree no matter how hard they tried.

Babes would throw a massive tantrum each time they failed, but Starr calmed her down by singing Babes's favourite advertising jingle (which was for a dishwasher tablet) and telling her little sister: 'We'll grow big soon.'

Sometimes, when the girls were very good, Mum would put the ladder against the tree so they could climb up to the treehouse.

It was the sisters' favourite place, and they could see the birdhouse in the park from there.

When summer was over,
Babes started school.
She was very excited.

She was going to the same
school as her big sister.

Starr helped her with her school bag.
'You look great, Babes,'
she told her sister.

And Babes said:
'Call me Barbara now.
I'm a big girl.'

Babes was right.
She was getting to be a big girl.

She was growing faster than Starr was.
And Starr knew why.

Starr had dwarfism.
That meant she would always
be a little person.
Mum had often talked to her about this.

Also, Starr had a special doctor,
who explained it all, and sometimes
she had to go to hospital.

Being a little person
had never made Starr sad before.

But then one day,
when she came home from school,
she saw that Babes (who got home
earlier) had climbed up to the treehouse,
even though Mum hadn't put up the ladder.

Starr asked her mother
if growing big was important,
thinking that Mum would say:
No, it's not important.

But Mum said:
'It's very important, sweetie.
There will be days when things feel just
too big for you to handle on your own.
But you will find ways to cope,
and I'll always be here to help.'

Starr started to cry, because she knew
that one of those days was coming
the very next week, at school.
And Mum would not be there to help.

Mum calmed her down
by singing Starr's favourite lullaby.

It was not an advertising jingle.
It was a special song Mum had made up
on the night Starr was born.

Reach for that star
Wherever you are.
Reach for that star
And see.

Reach for that star
No matter how far
And waiting up there
Is me.

'You don't need to worry,' said Mum,
when Starr's sobs had turned to sniffles.
'We love you, me and Babes both,
and that's what really matters.
We're tough enough and we're smart
enough to get through anything together.

'When you were born,
I could see the North Star
from the baby hospital window.
And that's why I named you Starr.
Because I thought that some day
you would reach for the star in our song.'

Starr stopped crying,
but she was sad for the rest of the day
because she thought now that
no matter how hard she tried,
she could never reach that star.

Starr had always loved school.

She could remember being a little nervous at first, but her teacher, Miss Emily, had been very kind, and Starr had made more than *twenty* new friends on her very first day.

For the first two years at school,
being a little person made no difference.
Starr was small, but so were her classmates.

She could reach
the coat-hooks,
which were
quite low.
And the bathroom
sinks were at the
perfect height.

But after that, when the class moved out of the junior corridor, everything was bigger.

The children grew bigger too, over the summer.
But not Starr.

She couldn't quite reach the top bookshelf, and her table was just a bit too high.

Her new teacher, Miss Sita,
moved Starr's coat-hook down a little.
She made sure Starr had a stepstool
to help her to reach things, and she
adjusted anything in the new classroom
that was too high for her.

But there were things
Miss Sita could not change.

The playground equipment
was too big for Starr.

She could not reach
the climbing bars in the
gym and the rungs on
the ladder were too
far apart.

But Starr remembered what
her mum had said:
There will always be days
when things feel just too big
for you to handle on your own.

And so she found other things
to do during break-time.

She ate her lunch
and fed the pigeons.

29

Starr knew Sports Day was coming soon.
She loved school,
but she did not love Sports Day.

Break-time was only thirty minutes long,
but Sports Day went on for hours.

Starr remembered her first Sports Day.
It was awful.
She didn't want to run in any of the races.
She couldn't do the hurdles.
And there was no way she was
climbing the rope.

She had spent the whole day feeling
so left out that she pretended to have
a tummy ache when Sports Day came
around again, so she could spend the
day at home.

And this year it was going to be even worse.

Starr's classmates were bigger now. They could run faster and reach further.

And this time Babes would be racing and jumping and climbing, too.

Babes, who wanted to be called Barbara, and was taller than Starr now.

I'm not a big sister any more, Starr thought.

33

Starr was a very clever girl,
but she couldn't think her way through
the problem of being small,
because it went on for ever.

She lay on her bed
and looked at the big glittering star
that Mum had painted on the wall
of the girls' room.

When Starr reached out her hand,
the star seemed further away
than it had been the day before.

Starr felt like being alone for a while
but Babes came into the room
and wanted to play.

'Play,' she demanded,
pressing on the mattress
until Starr bounced,
but Starr was not in a bouncing mood.

'No, Barbara,' said Starr. 'I'm sad.'

'I'm Babes today,' said her sister.
'Not Barbara.'

Babes had squashed herself into
her old onesie and tied her hair
into baby pigtails.

She pointed to her own face.
'*Babes,*' she said. 'Now play.'

And so they did play, like in the old days,
when Babes had been only three,
instead of the grown-up five she was now.

They played all their favourite games
and Starr forgot to be sad,
until Babes got too excited
and knocked Starr down by accident.

As she sat on the floor,
Starr began to cry again,
because for her being small was for ever.

Babes sat on the carpet beside her sister.
'Stop crying, Starr,' said Babes.
'We're playing. I'm Babes.'

Starr sniffed.
'No, Babes. You're Barbara now.
A big girl.'

'I don't want to be big,' said Babes.
'*You're* big. My big sister.'

Starr wished she was a big sister.
She really wished and wanted it
but it would be less true every day.

'I am your big sister,' she said at last.
'Your *little* big sister.'

And Starr sang the dishwasher tablet song
until Babes fell asleep on the floor.

Next day, Starr decided to stay in bed.

'You have to get dressed, Starr,'
said Mum. 'You'll be late for school.'

'I have a tummy ache,' said Starr,
even though her tummy was fine.

'Oh,' said Mum. 'Maybe you need
a cuddle.'

Mum climbed into Starr's bed and they lay there cuddling until Starr said: 'You shouldn't have called me Starr, because I'll never be able to reach the star.'

'You don't just reach with your arms,' said Mum. 'You reach with your mind and your talents. Whenever you have a clever idea, or use one of your talents, you reach for that star.'

43

'I still have a tummy ache,' said Starr.

'I know, honey,' said Mum.
'And you still have to go to school
this week, even though Sports Day
is tomorrow.'

Starr was upset.
'But all I do is stand around
with nothing to do.'

'I know that happened before,' said Mum.
'But I think it will go better this year.
I've had a word with Miss Sita already,
and she's had a word with the principal.'

'And...?' said Starr.

'You just get dressed, sweetie, unless
you really do have a tummy ache.'

Starr threw back the quilt
and climbed out of bed.

When Miss Sita came into the classroom she had an important announcement for the class.

'I have noticed,' she said,
'that not everyone enjoys Sports Day.
So we are setting up a Triple A
near the racing track tomorrow.'

'What's a Triple A?' Starr asked.

'A Triple A is an Alternative Activities Area,' said Miss Sita. 'The activities will be supervised by volunteers.'

'What *are* the alternative activities?' asked someone else.

Miss Sita didn't know the answer to that one just yet.
'We'll find out tomorrow,' she said.

The next day, when Mum
brought the girls to school,
Starr saw the other kids
all limbering up for their events.
She felt herself getting sad again.

Mum looked at Starr and said,
'Remember, Starr, you are multi-faceted.
That means –'

'I know,' said Starr.
'We did this one before.
It means I am lots of different things
all mixed together.'

'That's right, my clever girl,' said Mum.
'You are smart and funny
and quick and imaginative and cheeky.
And *also* you are a little person.'

'Everyone starts out little,' said Starr
sadly. 'But I'm little *for ever.*'

'Don't think about for ever,
sweetie,' said Mum.
'Just think about today.
And remember, every
day when you come
home, no matter how
hard the day has been,
Babes and I will be
here for you.'

Babes ran off to the racing track, but Starr wanted to explore the Triple A.

It was wonderful.

There was a reading area,
with stools and beanbags
from the junior corridor.
That area was supervised by...
Mum, in a yellow vest.

There was a chill zone where
people could get some shade
and even take a nap.

There was a chefs' corner where children could make their very own pancakes.

There was a board games section, running a Monopoly competition.

There was a fitness area,
where children could exercise
with someone's grandad,
who used to be a gym teacher.

And best of all, there was
a skate run where skateboarders
could practise on a slalom course.

Starr tried all the alternative activities.

And she wasn't the only one.

There were lots of children
who couldn't take part
in the main Sports Day events,
and a few who didn't enjoy sports
and would prefer to read.

Luckily, Mum had remembered
to bring Starr's favourite thing –
her skateboard. So Starr spent
most of the day in the skate run.

She had a brilliant time doing kick-turns
and ollies between the cones.

Every now and then, Starr took a break from skateboarding, to watch the races and cheer Babes on.

Babes was extremely fast.
She almost came third in the sack race, and she won the egg-and-spoon race.

She got a trophy in the shape
of an egg-cup.

That made everyone laugh.

Starr got a trophy too.

She was one of only three children
to complete the slalom run
on their skateboards
without knocking over a single cone.

They all got trophies
in the shape of a star.

'Stand with your big sister, Babes,'
said Mum. 'And hold up your trophies.
I want to take a picture of
my two champions.'

Starr smiled and moved
her hand a little until
the sunlight caught
the gold star trophy
and made it twinkle
in her eyes.

She knew that tomorrow she might find that some toilet was too high or that she couldn't reach a door handle somewhere.

But that was tomorrow, and Mum had said, *Just think about today.*

Starr was happy to think about today. She knew this was a day she would never forget.

Because today she had not felt left out. Not for a single second.

Later that evening, when Starr
had finished reading Babes
her third bedtime story,
Mum asked Starr if she
had reached that star
in her lullaby today.

And today,
for the first time ever,
Starr could say...

yes!

About the Author

Eoin Colfer is the author of the internationally bestselling *Artemis Fowl*, which was voted the public's favourite Puffin Classic of all time and was made into a Disney movie. Other titles include *The Wish List*, *The Supernaturalist* and the *Legends* series for younger readers. Eoin's books have won numerous awards including the British Children's Book of the Year, the Irish Book Awards Children's Book of the Year and the German Children's Book of the Year. The BBC made a hit series based on his book *Half Moon Investigations*. In 2009, Eoin was commissioned by Douglas Adams's estate to write *And Another Thing*, the concluding episode of the *Hitchhiker's Guide to the Galaxy* series, which became a worldwide bestseller.

Eoin has collaborated with Irish artists PJ Lynch, Oliver Jeffers and Chris Judge on a series of award-winning picture books. Eoin has written the book for the musicals *The Lords of Love* and *Noël* with composer Liam Bates. Eoin was Ireland's third Children's Laureate and still wears the medal at all times, even in the bath.

About the Illustrator

Celia Ivey is a Cornish-French illustrator born with dwarfism, currently based in Bristol, UK. She attained her BA (Hons) in Visual Communcation & Illustration at the University of West London.

Aside from her love of brightly-coloured jumpers and a tendency to laugh at her own jokes, she is passionate about visual storytelling and spends her time immersed in a vibrant world of pop art, comics, and 1950's animation.

Celia works exclusively on an iPad Pro, using the 'Procreate' app, as she finds it to be the most accessible medium, and it greatly facilitates her ability to produce finished work. As a disabled artist, Celia has a unique perspective that is invaluable to produce nuanced storytelling, combined with her ever-present love of vibrant colour.

About Little Island Books

Little Island Books is an independent Irish children's press that publishes the best new writing for young readers.
To find out more about Little Island you can visit littleisland.ie

Little Island
Books create waves